The Brogan Book:

Thoughts of Thomas

By Thomas Brogan

ISBN: 978-1-4116-8-8506-2

To my family and friends: Thank you for putting up with me over the years.

blar·ney [**blahr**-nee]: deceptive or misleading talk; nonsense; hooey

sar·casm [**sahr**-kaz-*uh*m]: harsh or bitter derision or irony.

Brogan's Mind

Enter At Your Own Risk

Ideas, Rants, Accusations, Thoughts, Sarcasm and lots of Blarney.

Good Morning

Does anyone else ever get sick out saying good morning? I do. I have noticed lately that people are getting so lazy with the phrase that they just say "morning". No "good", just the "morning". How am I suppose to respond to this? Should I just say " Thanks Captain Obvious", because I already know that it's the morning.

Breakfast Cereal

I am curious if I am the only one who does this? After I pour a bowl of cereal into the bowl I put the box down next to me at the table. If I have no paper to read, I will read the entire cereal box, from nutritional information to ingredients. I do this everytime I eat cereal. I could have the same box of Lucky Charms for a week straight and still read that stupid box everytime I eat it........If you ask me to remember what it says......no clue! Somehow when I eat cereal, my brain goes to a far off galaxy where it can't retain information. Can anyone else relate?

Caught in the Act

I know other people do this. It just can't be me. The other day I was sitting at dinner, I wondered to myself if I remembered to put on deodorant that morning. It is such a habit to slap on deodorant, sometimes I don't realize that I do it. So I decided to check this little problem out. I did the "fake turn" over my left shoulder and pretended to look at something. Little did everyone else know, I was really smelling for B.O. The left pit smelled good, now I had to check out the right one. But, I just couldn't do the same "fake turn" again, so I decided to do the "fake stretch". I raised up my arms in the air and tilted my head to the right. Ahhhh...Smells like Right Guard to me. Just then my dinner companion called me on it. She had realized what I was doing. Man, did I feel like an idiot. But we all do it.....DON'T WE?

Are Those Real?

I think I know what it feels like to be a woman with fake breasts. How can this be possible? I get asked on a daily basis, "Are those real?" Yes they are and thank you for asking. Of course this comment is being directed towards my eyes not, my breasts. It is nice to be complimented on something......but when that is the only thing you hear, over and over again.....it gets old. I know that there are many others of you out there. You have the perfect hair, the perfect butt, or something that everyone always makes a comment on. It is strange how someone trying to be nice to you can actually annoy you.

Rain, Rain Go Away

It's amazing how some people are so afraid to get wet? They act as if liquid hot magma is falling from the sky and is going to burn them. No folks, it's just harmless water drops. Oh, it may mess up the hair a bit, but overall you will be okay. So instead of running like wild beasts across the parking lot dashing in front of cars........Take your time, take on a little water and walk safely, avoiding cars and other moving objects. Besides, the messy look for hair is in..... isn't it?

Wet Plastic = Anger

I don't ask for too many things in my life. But for once, I would like to open up my dishwasher and see a new sight. All I want is to have my tupperware and other plastic items be dry! Everytime, it's the same old thing. I pick up the piece of tupperware and water dribbles all over. Either that or there is a big puddle on top of my favorite plastic Iowa State mug. What I don't understand is...... It has an option for "Heated Dry". Shouldn't this take care of the problem? I know this isn't an isolated event. I have used over 10 dishwashers, all with the same effect.

If someone knows of a dishwasher, that guarantees to dry tupperware please let me know! I am willing to pay large sums of money and maybe even my first born child. Just help me get a piece of dry tupperware!!!

The Bathroom

Have you ever been on the same bathroom schedule as someone else? What exactly do I mean by this? It seems like everytime I go and use the bathroom throughout the day, I run into the same few people. It never fails. I know walking in that I will see certain individuals. So this means that they are always in the bathroom or we are just on the same schedule. While I am on the subject of bathrooms, I think most men can relate to this one. You walk into a bathroom and there can be at least 10 urinals lined up across the wall. They are all empty. I walk to the very end urinal to do my business and it never fails. The next guy to walk in has the option of 8 other urinals that are not right next to me, but he chooses the one at my side. I can't figure this one out.

Weight Loss Plan

I have a question to pose. On television ads featuring weight loss plans, why do the before and after picture look so different? I understand that the person should look a lot slimmer. But what about the other changes? I mean, does a tanning package and a bottle of hair dye come with the "wonder" fat-burning pills? Take some time and look the next time you see one of these commercials. In the before picture: A tired looking, pale, dark haired fat woman wearing sweats and a t-shirt. In the after picture: A tan, skinny, blond haired woman in a swimsuit. Come on!
At least make it look realistic. That is an easy lawsuit waiting to happen. I am going to take the pills and when I don't get tan and end up on a beach somewhere, with blond highlights, I am going to cry "False Advertising". Then I will win my lawsuit, eat steak all the time and get fat. But, the ironic thing is, there will be no fat burning pills to take, because I will have forced the company out of business with my lawsuit.

Changing Lanes

Lately getting around town has been a little more difficult with all of the construction going on. But, what really makes it difficult is some of the other drivers out there. It seems like sometimes when you merge onto the interstate you are entering a thunderdome, with no rules or regulations.
There are bascially five types of people driving the roads:

1.) The Average Joe - These are people such as myself who obey basic traffic laws and that have a little bit of common sense.
2.) The Soccer Mom - These are moms who are usually driving an SUV or Mini-Van around town. Their cargo....Kids, Lots of them. They are known for showing a soccer ball emblem in their back window. You must be aware of the Soccer Mom because she is trying to operate a large vehicle with kids screaming, a DVD movie showing while talking on the cell phone.
3.)The Old Timers - Yes, we should respect our elders, but at the same time, we should fear them as well. The Old Timers drive around town, usually in their oversized Cadillacs going 10 miles under the posted speed limit. Sometimes you can't even see them because they can't see over the steering wheel. You must take caution when driving next to them because they believe for some reason that they have earned the right to drive in two lanes.
4.) The Out-Of-Towners - Yes we have all been one, at one time or another. They have the habit of driving really slow when looking for their destination. They go the wrong way down one ways and seem to have a bewildered look in their eyes at all times.
5.) Road Ragers - This is the most dangerous of the group. These are people who for some reason are mad at the world. They like to drive at outrageous speeds while swerving in and out of lanes. When you are trying to merge and see a Road Rager, forget it. They will not let you in! They will speed up, slow down and do whatever it takes to block you out. If you do somehow manage to get in front of them, they will ride your tail, honk and even flip the old bird to get you out of their path.

The Casino

The Casino: The Land of opportunity, smoke, addiction, fun, horse racing and slots.
When do you think slot machines will start accepting social security checks? Have you been out there lately? I personally go to the casino every so often and have a great time. But, there are others who hang out there all the time. I lot of eldery folks hang out there both day and night. I don't know if the casino is suppose to double for a retired home, but it looks that way. The other day when I was there I saw a lady in a wheelchair playing the slots. Right next to her... an oxygen tank. In her mouth.....a cigarette. I was shocked! She is one of many eldery folks who daily spend their pention and social security checks in the slots. They just want to see that "777". The eldery seem to be the only ones winning out there. Of course if you sit at one machine feeding it hundreds and hundreds of quarters you are bound to win.
I never seem to win out there. Someday I am going to test the theory that only the eldery win out there. I am going to dress up as an old person and use a wheelchair. I will wave at the cameras with my wrinkled fingers and then play. I guarantee I will win. No doubt about it!

The Drive-Thru

Does anyone else do this? When you are going thru a drive-thru and you receive your food, the drive-thru employee says "Enjoy your food". Then out of habit you say "You too!" But they aren't going to eat the food. It just goes to show we don't think before we talk.

The European Dream

I recently read a book about the European Dream. The book talks about how in today's world people are no longer looking to achieve the so called "American Dream". The American Dream originally was based on the idea of life, liberty and the pursuit of happiness. Today's American dream is something totally different. In America we live a fast paced life with very litte rest and only pursue material possesions. I see this to be true here in the midwest. Look at all the new homes going up in all the suburbs. You have 5 bedroom houses that only 2 people live in. Half the time the people who live in the house can't afford to buy furniture for the inside the house they just spent a half million for. If you look in the paper you can see that the amount of bankruptcies are on the rise.
So what is this European Dream? In Europe they live a more relaxed, slow paced life. They are known to take 2-3 hour lunches and leave early from work. They are granted extended vacations and maternity leave from work. Europeans don't worry about keeping up with their neighbors. They take value not in possessions but with spending time with family and friends.
I think the European Dream sounds good. I think we all need to take a few ideas from this and life in America would be much better!

No Thanks

The other day I was eating dinner with a friend and she had ordered a specialty drink. I could tell by the looks of the drink that it wasn't going to taste that good in the first place. She tried it and said that it tasted nasty. She then told me to try it................................Wait a minute.

You said the drink was nasty, but now you want me to try it? Why would I want to try something that was nasty? Have you ever noticed that people do this all the time. I have done it. I get some food that tastes a litte bit off and I always offer it to someone else to try. Why do we do this?

Opening Your Eyes

I was talking to one of my friends the other day and we both agreed on something. When you are kissing someone, one of the weirdest feelings is opening your eyes and seeing another set of eyes staring back at you. Most people kiss with their eyes shut, this seems normal to me. It is just plain creepy to see someone just staring at you during a make out session. Some food for thought!

Cell Phones

It seems like everybody and their mom has a cell phone. I have had one since the early days when the phone was pretty much bigger than my face. I think by now most people are use to seeing and hearing people all around them talking on their phones. But, after all these years of being desensitized to the cell phone chatter around me, I still can't get over what some people will say. You can be right behind them in line at the supermarket and they will be talking about a lesbian threesome they just had the night before. Okay they don't talk about that, but the subjects that some people talk about, I don't want to hear.

Then there are the loud talkers. You know what I mean. They shout into the cell phone. Sometimes I think some of these people shout so that we can hear their conversations. They talk about how many stocks they have, how much they just made off a deal, whatever it takes to impress us. Here is some news for you........I don't care about what your friend Shirley thinks about something or what new car you just bought. I just want to get through the check out line without hearing your stupid conversation.

Plus, you get the ones that stay on the phone while they are trying to get something done. They walk up to pay for their groceries and they stay on the phone. No hello to the cashier, no nothing. How rude! I don't think people should get served in a store until they hang up the phone.

So the next time you are using the phone where everybody can hear you....please either lower your voice (to a normal level) or wait five minutes and call the person back when you get into your car. A little bit of courtesy goes a long way.

Chicken Nuggets

I just got home from picking up some food at Wendy's. I love Wendy's because they have the 99 cent menu that includes a 5 piece chicken nugget. For some reason though, everytime I order the nuggets I say "chicken mcnuggets", which we all know is what McDononald's calls them. I stop and try again but I can't not say "mc" in front of the nugget. Am I the only one who does this?

The Parking Ramp

I was running right on time today for work. When I say right on time I mean I will sit down at my desk, right at 8am. Then I hit the parking ramp. On any other day, this would have been no problem. But today I had been caught up in some heavy traffic so I was cutting it a bit close. I would definately have to put some pride in my stride and haul my butt fast through the skywalk.
So I pull into the gate at the bottom of the ramp. Usually around this time everybody else is putting in that extra effort and have already made it to their desk, so the ramp is all mine. Nope......not today. I have a mini van that has pulled into the gate right before me. The stalls are right next to each other and both lead up into the ramp. I know I need to beat this car. I could tell that this would be a very slow person. At this point the mini van and my car are lined up like two horses ready to run the race of a life time. I put my card in, it does not work. I try again......nothing. I look over and see the gate going up for the van. I knew it was over.
After a few minute of messing with my parking card I finally got it to work. I could still see the van in front of me going at least one mile per hour. WHY!!!
Have you ever been behind one of these people in a ramp. There is no room to go around them. You are just out of luck. They go really slow making sure they don't miss that heaven sent parking spot. Then sometimes they see a spot, which they really can't fit into. You can see that they won't fit, I am sure they can see it, but they try it anyway. They pull in half way, then pull out, then pull in once more, then finally give up. All that time you are waiting behind them. Sometimes something as easy as parking is a mystery to some people.
On a brighter note, I did somehow make it to work right on time.

Freezing In Iowa

You know what Iowa needs? Some bitterly cold weather.......Oh yeah go outside, it is -30 degrees out!

What were the early Iowa settlers thinking when they decided to just stop going west and stay in Iowa. It couldn't of been during the winter. Can you image that? It is -30 degrees out, they didn't have coats or clothes like we have today. Can you really see someone saying " Well, I can't feel my hands, my nose hairs are freezing, little Billy's face is turning blue, let's start a new life here."

The Christmas Pounds

Tis the season to gain those unwanted pounds. The biggest reason we gain the pounds has to be the holiday sweets. Everywhere you look there are cookies, fudge and candy that you can't say no to. My office is the worst place for temptation. You can easily find a treat whenever you need one or don't need one. Well I won't be bringing in treats this year. I have come up with a new idea.

I am cutting out the middleman (cookies, candy, fudge). I am just going to bring in a can of lard and some spoons. I figure if I want to just get fat, I will just eat plain fat. Why not? Why go to all that trouble beating eggs and frosting cookies, the end result will be the same either way. Besides, no matter what you bring in to the office, if it's free, people will eat it. You ever notice that?

So join with me this holiday season and enjoy a can of lard!

Gift Cards

A lot of people are giving gift cards now as gifts. I for one don't mind getting the gift card. This means I can get what I want to and not have to wear that purple sweater with the pear design on it that my grandma picks out for me.

The one weird thing about the gift card is when I am shopping normally without one I can find at least a thousand things that I want to buy. But once I enter that store with the gift card in hand (free money to burn), I can't seem to find one thing I want. Since I have no patience I feel that I have to spend it that day! I can't wait. I have money to spend, which doesn't happen to often. I usually end up buying something that I really didn't want or need just to use the gift card up........... I wonder if this happens to anyone else??

The Refrigerator

I arrived home late last night and I was feeling hungry. I knew before I opened the refrigerator that there wasn't going to be much in there. But, I figured that I might as well check. I opened the door and I saw a great condiment selection and some beer. That wan't going to feed my hunger. I closed the door and sat down on my couch............. 5 Minutes go by................another 10 minutes................... I still haven't eaten anything............ I am still very much hungry.
So I head into the kitchen again. I decide to take another look in the fridge, thinking that someway food will magically appear in there. Still nothing. I ended up going through this process 4 times before I finally just gave up and went to bed.

Am I the only one that does this? I think not. I know that there are many people out there that take that look into the fridge more than just once, some how thinking that the food fairy will deliver you some food.

Suitcase on Wheels

Have you seen these people that take luggage to work with them? You know those suitcases on wheels that you can pull behind you. What are these people bringing to work? Their paperweight collection? What can really be that heavy that you would need a suitcase?
To me this would be too much like going on vacation. I think if I started taking luggage to work it would totally ruin my whole vacation experience. Every time I was pulling my suitcase in the airport it would feel like I am going to work! Who wants that?

Mall Parking

The holiday season is upon us and once again we all must head to the mall to shop. My biggest problem with going shopping has to be the parking. Finding a close spot when it is only 12 degrees outside is key to any shopping mission.
When pulling into the parking lot you first look for those coveted empty spots in the front rows. Since this never happens you usually have to look for people walking out to their car so you can take their spot. You slowly cruise and follow these people hoping that they will be in one of those great spots. I call this "parking spot stalking". Sometimes when I am walking out of the mall I like to mess with people who are following me for my spot. I like to stop at the car in the spot closest to the entrance. I pretend to be looking for my keys while the person in the car waits. You know that the "parking spot stalker" is feeling giddy because their parking prayer has been answered. They sit there and wait. Then after a few minutes of this, I stop and walk to my car parked in the back of the lot.
Another big thing that bugs me with parking at the mall is the spots that you think are empty, but really they're not. Those small cars (Geo Metro, etc.) always get me. They are usually parked in between two big suvs. You are going along thinking you see the empty spot and sometimes even start to pull in before....BAM, you have to slam on the breaks. All dreams are destroyed by that stupid small car. You might have been fooled also by the cart holders and those spots that have a tree in the middle of them.
Holiday shopping is stressful enough, maybe more malls need valet parking. I would rather pay money then deal with finding a spot and walking in the cold. But that is just one man's opinion.

Second to None

I came up with a brilliant idea this past weekend. For some reason I kept hearing the phrase "Second to None", on the radio and on television commercials. For some reason all these companies think that they are the best. This got me thinking......
Somebody should start a business named "None". Think about it, it is a marketing gold mine. Everytime an ad says that they are "Second to None", they are actually admitting that your company, "None", is the best. You are #1. They are second to only you.

The Scar of Marriage

All of my friends are getting married! I could warn them not to do it, but I won't. Just because I got married when I was 19 in Vegas and it didn't work out (no I wasn't drunk) , doesn't mean all marriage is bad. Let's take a look at some marriage wisdom......

-By all means marry. If you get a good wife, you'll be happy. If you get a bad one, you'll become a philosopher...and that is a good thing for any man.
-A successful man is one who makes more money than his wife can spend. A successful woman is one who can find such a man.
-Marriage is a great institution, but I'm not ready for an institution.
-Marriage is a three ring circus: engagement ring, wedding ring, and suffering.
-Marriage is the triumph of imagination over intelligence. Second marriage is the triumph of hope over experience.
-Marriage is when a man and woman become as one, the trouble starts when they try to decide which one.
-Marriages are made in heaven. But so again, are thunder and lightning.
-Do not marry a person that you know you can live with, only marry someone that you cannot live without.

The Forbidden Call

Has this ever happened to you? You're on the phone with a friend, having a good conversation, sharing funny stories, when out of no where you hear................ a very familiar sound....................... the sound of............yeah that sounds like................it can't be.................. yes, a stream of liquid falling into a body of water.................. they are going to the bathroom while on the phone.

A few thoughts about this. First, I don't care how close I am to you, I don't want to hear it!!!!!! It only takes a minute to give me a call back, I will understand if you have to urinate.

Now, I can let the old #1 go most of the time. But please don't even think about using the phone during the #2. This is just wrong. This gives a whole new meaning to a "shitty conversation". I don't want any part of it. Not only should you not be on the phone during this process, but the phone shouldn't even be in the bathroom.

Creepy Burger King Commercial

Is it just me, or is anyone else freaked out by the "King" in the Burger King Commercials. In the ad they show people waking up to the king's face in their window and being all happy. If I woke up to a giant plastic face with a smirk on it, I would bash it in with a bat. It reminds me of Michael Myers from Halloween.

More Weird BK Stuff

Burger King has out done themselves. First they had the weird looking King with the huge plastic head. Now something that I thought would never be scary. Let me say that I love Chicken Fingers. I could eat them everyday. So the Burger King commercial for the "Chicken Fries" was quite disturbing. First they show a picture of these new chicken fries. Yummy, looks good right? Then they flash to a band with giant chicken heads on, jumping about and playing their guitars in an old factory. This looks like something out of a horrible nightmare. Chickens running around.....this should only be happening if they have had their heads cut off....right? If you haven't seen this, look for it on the tube. Warning...you might be disturbed.

Cold But Hot

You scream, I scream we all scream for ice cream..........

I was eating some ice cream the other day which in it self is weird because when it is negative Iowa degrees out, who wants something cold. But, I was craving it, so I scooped out a few scoops of vanilla ice cream in a bowl. I got some of the vanilla heaven in my spoon and before I took the bite, I blew on the ice cream......Hmmmmmm...Why did I do this? Ice cream is cold, not hot. I noticed that I did this a few other times during my domination of the ice cream. Am I crazy?...or do other people actually have some kind of brain association between eating something with a spoon and thinking it will be hot.

Race Car Drivers On the Streets

Have you noticed the people who put race car stickers on their cars? You know they have an "8" or some sort of Jeff Gordon sign. I think these people actually think once that sticker is placed on their car, they have the right to drive like one of the drivers. They speed, change lanes without warning, ride your tail and are just plain annoying. These are the people that cause road rage. AHHHHHHHHHHH!!

On another note.... This is nothing against anyone who watches Nascar. But, I really don't see how you can watch that for hours on T.V. It is just a bunch of cars going around in a circle hundreds of times. How is this fun to watch?

Captain Obvious Award Winner

Have you seen these signs while driving around town? (See picture below) Do they really need to be posted? This easily gets the "Thanks, Captain Obvious" Award for the year. Shouldn't we just know that you love your kids? Do you really need a sign stating the fact? Will this sign stop someone from driving fast?.........NO! You think some road rage driver doing 65mph in your neighborhood is going to see the sign and think to themselves, "Wow, I should slow down, these people love their kids. I will wait until I get to the next neighborhood without a sign, where they hate their kids, to speed up and finish my beer."

Winter Driving

Usually when the roads have been covered with ice most people drive with a little more caution. Everyone except the SUV owners. They seem to think that somehow because they have an SUV that they can just drive through anything. Here's a news bulletin for ya: 4 Wheel Drive doesn't really help you out on ice. So when you are doing 65 on a side street covered with ice riding my butt you might not be able to stop.

I don't mean this in a bad way, I don't want to see anyone hurt, but over 50 percent of the vehicles you see in the ditchs are SUVs (this makes me laugh). Hmmmmmmm.......... Maybe they should slow down a bit?

The Movies

I went to see a movie the other night. Going through the concession stand there reminded me of something. Why do people eat nachos at the movies. Nachos are just too loud of a food to eat during a movie. The last thing I want to hear every two minutes during the movie is the sound of a crunching chip. The other thing that bugs me about the movie theater experience are the arm rests. Which one am I suppose to use? Shouldn't there be some unwritten law about this. If everyone would just say the left one is yours, then you wouldn't have to worry about it. But there are always the few that think they are entitled to both of them. This is when I would love to take my jumbo $12.00 soda and "accidently" spill it over there arm on my arm rest.

Chicken Fingers

I will go on record as saying that Chicken fingers are my favorite food in the world. You can't go wrong with them. It is pretty much a safe bet at any restaurant. I mean how hard are they to make. Sure there are some better than others, but if you are dipping them in ranch, they are all wonderful. I am really convinced that you could dip poop in ranch dressing and it would taste good. But that is neither here nor there.

I really don't understand though why they call them "fingers". I can see the resemblence with a finger (a big fat one), but usually when I hear finger, I don't think yummy to my tummy. So why name them fingers? I looked up the definition of a chicken finger and hear is what I found.

Chicken fingers - also known as chicken strips or chicken tenders, this is one of the most common forms of fried chicken, generally pieces of chicken breast (sometimes with rib meat) cut into long strips, breaded or batter-dipped, and deep fried.

So that doesn't answer my question. Hmmm. I guess I will have to chalk it up as one of life's great mysteries. I will go on eating my fingers, still never knowing.

The Red Hat Ladies

Have you seen the red hat ladies around town? Groups of older women get together wearing bright red hats. Why you ask? A very good question. After doing some research, here is what I found out:

"The Red Hat Society began as a result of a few women deciding to greet middle age with verve, humor and elan. We believe silliness is the comedy relief of life, and since we are all in it together, we might as well join red-gloved hands and go for the gusto together. Underneath the frivolity, we share a bond of affection, forged by common life experiences and a genuine enthusiasm for wherever life takes us next."

Although some of you might think that the red hat ladies are silly looking or stupid for wearing these attention getting hats, I think they are on to something. I think I need to start some sort of organization where men can get together and live life to the fullest! But what?

I know. I will start the Red Ski Mask Society for Men over 25. We will get together and just have fun and not take life seriously. We can go to the bar, go bowling, golf and much more. We could even run simple errands together. If brother Bob needed to go to the grocery store we would go. If he needed to go to the bank, our group of Red Ski Mask guys would go.

Written 10 days later........
So, we had our first get together yesterday. It didn't go so well. Brother Hernando needed some gas, so we all went to the local Git and Go. While he was pumping some gas the group of us wearing our ski masks decided to go inside and get some slushies. As soon as we walked in, everybody started screaming. I thought they were just excited that we formed a new club. But then an alarm went off and the teenage boy behind the counter pulled out a shotgun.

Written 30 days later......
After spending a little over a month in prison, I decided that the Red Ski Mask Society would not work out. For some reason the local police just wouldn't believe our story. But having a month to think about things, I think we would be better off just sticking with our weekly poker games to have fun as men. Hind Sight is 20/20!

The Streak

This year a thing to remember went down.
He was like a king, he could wear a crown.

It's hard to believe how he lasted so long.
While others have been injured, he went on.

He broke a record, a record that was sacred.
He streaked across the field two minutes, buck-naked!

I Have to Pee Like a Racehorse

I have said it. I have heard others say it. But what the hell does it really mean and why do we say it? I searched the net for an answer:

Why do we say, I have to pee like a race horse?

"Racehorses are commonly given Lasix (aka Salix) which is a powerful diuretic. They pee a lot right before they race, we're talking gallons and gallons. The medication is thought to help prevent nasal bleeding, which sometimes happens when racehorses supremely over-exert themselves."

Gallons of pee? Wow, that is a lot to hold in!

Thanks to Spell Check, I Can't Spell

I consider myself a pretty smart person. That being said, I really can't spell very well anymore. It takes a lot of thought to spell out a complicated word in my head. Why is this?...... I blame Spell Check. Yes, you know that nice little red line underneath all those misspelled words on your computer? I am to the point now where I am so dependent on that "little red line" that I don't even think about a word I am spelling correctly because I know it will be fixed for me. So in theory, this great invention of spell check is actually hurting society more than it's helping. So in one way, I have to worry about our future. With all the advancements in technology and humans having to use our brains less, will we resort back to our cavemen days? It will be interesting to see.

Just Driving

Today was just like any other day while driving to work. I was listening to some tunes, spacing off and trying not to be blinded by the sun. Then, I saw something. It was car transporter. But, this one was empty. The wheel tracks leading up to the back of the truck didn't look that far from the ground. It looked as if I could just drive my Ion right up it. I starting thinking to myself.... I should try it. Why should I do the same boring thing everyday? TODAY, I AM GOING TO GET CRAZY!!

So I floored my little 4-cylinder Saturn Ion (I felt like Tom Cruise in Days of Thunder). I was determined to get onto the back of the car transporter. My wheels met with the back of the truck, a horrible metal on metal screaching sound pierced my ears. I lost control of the car and did a 360 onto the otherside of the interstate. Wow. I guess the little Ion couldn't handle it. But at least I gave it a shot. :) I can't wait to explain this one to the insurance guy.

The Weather

I was listening to the radio this morning and they starting giving the weather report. They starting off by saying "Today it will be hot and humid." Thanks captain obvious! Do they really need to tell us that anymore? It is hot and humid everyday day during the summer in Iowa. I am not a genious or a meteriologist, but I will go out on a limb......... It will be hot and humid throughout August. WOW! What a bold statement. I am not going to give away a snowblower if I am wrong like a meteorologist, but maybe if I am wrong I will buy you a Bomb Pop.

Golf

I went golfing the other day. What a beautiful day for golf! The highlight of the day was almost hitting a Police Car as it drove by on the highway. I think the worst part of golf is that first hole. Today there were 4 other groups behind us waiting to tee off. That means they are all watching you....waiting for you to totally screw up. Well, at least that's how I am as I am watching the person in front of me. Either you hit it well and you can take a slow walk to your cart, with your head up high.... or you totally shank the ball or miss it totally and walk quickly to your cart with your head down praying that no one noticed. Today, thank God, I made some good contact!

You've really got a MOLD on me.

Yesterday I made myself a nice BLT sandwich (Crisp bacon, crunchy lettuce and garden fresh tomatoes). It tasted great! Today I grabbed the bread from the bread box and what did I see?............ MOLD!!!! Could this mold have been there yesterday when I ate the BLT? Did it just grow overnight? I suddenly started to feel sick to my stomach. The BLT sandwich tasted good enough. Wouldn't I have noticed if there was mold on the bread?
Isn't it amazing how our minds work against us? I don't know for sure if I ate mold or not, but just the thought of it made me want to throw up in my mouth. Have you ever seen something after that the fact with food? Maybe you noticed that the milk was out of date after you drink it. How did you react?

The Checkout Line

It doesn't matter where I am, it could be Target, Hy-Vee, Dahl's, or Wal-Mart, whenever I pick a line it turns out to be the slowest. There could be 20 people in the line next to me and only 2 in the lane I am at. But some how, those 20 people get through before I do. It FRUSTRATES ME!
The little light above the counter that is lit up......as soon as I enter that lane it starts blinking. I don't know if I just have the worst luck ever or what!
The worst is when you get that person who doesn't think the price came up right. They sit there and argue because the Bounty Paper Towels came up as $1.10 instead of $1.00. That is when I pull a dime out of my pocket slam it on the counter and say please move on in life. It is only a dime!

Thank you Target

One of the most valuable things I get from Target each week isn't the groceries I buy, but the plastic bags they come in. This is true of plastic bags from any grocery store. I prefer Target bags because they are a little heavier quality, but that is neither here nor there. The point is..... You can use them for just about anything. Here is just a short list of the wonders of the Target plastic bag. The main thing I use them for is my daily lunch sack. They are perfect. Each day you see the work fridge lined with different grocery store bags. They are so much cooler than paper bags! Okay, here are some other ways to recycle your plastic bags:
1. Use them for cleaning the litter box
2. Use them as a trash can liner in a small garbage can
3. Make a new outfit with them (see picture)
4. Use them to put your old soda cans in
5. They make perfect cat toys (my kitten can't get enough)
6. Use them for taking clothes to the good will
7. Do you have a new pair of shoes and it is raining...No problem, use the sacks to put over your shoes to protect them.
8. If you are a professional hitman, you can use them to suffocate your victims
9. They make a perfect parachute for hamsters!
10. Use them to take clothes to the laundry mat
11. And last but now least...... They are great to vomit in.

Thanks Target! We should be paying for these sacks.

A Dog's World

Cigarettes are a dog, man's best friend.
They both are by your side until the end.

They both can be a way of getting out your stress.
They both can smell very bad and make a huge mess.

Panburger Partner

Let me start off by saying that I am a cheap skate. I don't get wrapped up in all of the marketing hype behind name brands. I know just like many of you that most of the same products are made at the same plant and shipped away with two different labels. One name brand and the other "Brand X". So if I see something that is cheaper and looks the same I will buy it. A classic example..... Hamburger Helper. I am a Hy Vee Man. They are by far my favorite super market. Along with Hamburger Helper, they have there own brand called Panburger Partner. Folks, if you look at the ingredients....It's the same thing! You are paying extra for Hamburger Helper's ad campaign. So the next time you are at the store and have a choice between a name brand and "Brand X", save yourself some money and put your pride to the side!

Uncomfortable Return

Well, I did it again this morning. I seem to fall into the same trap on a daily basis. A trap set by my self. I opened the door to my car this morning to head for work. Of course I was only half awake (like a zombie pretty much). I slowly put the key in and started the Ion up. Then.............. BLAST!!!!!!!!!!!!!!!! No it wasn't a car bomb planted by a member of the Corleone family, it was my radio turned up to a point where it felt like my ears were going to bleed. What was I thinking when I pulled my car into the garage the night before?
Isn't it strange that the music didn't seem so loud the night before, but now it just made me insane in the membrane. Another one of life's mysteries. I guess I could just get in the habit of turning off the radio when I leave the car..... But that would be too easy.

Movie Time Fear

Have you ever been to a movie where you are the only person there? This happens a lot of times when you go to a movie in the afternoon during the week. It is like having your own private screening room. You can put your feet up and relax, not have to worry about anybody talking..... and then......at the last second, somebody else walks into the theater. All is lost! I don't mind as much if the person sits in front of me. Then at least I can see what they are up to. If they sit behind me then I am just plain paranoid. I always have this fear that they are going to come up from behind me and slit my throat. I guess I have seen too many scary movies. It could be a 98 year old grandma and in my mind I would be thinking of Norman Bates (Psycho) dressing up like his old mom killing people!

Navy Sock or Black Sock?

Am I the only person who can't tell the difference between navy blue socks and black socks? When I'm at the store sometimes I just can't tell by looking, I have to look at the tag to find out the color. Of course I can usually tell the difference really fast when I'm at work wearing black pants and notice my socks don't match. Then I feel really cool.

Engagement Conspiracy?

The more and more I think about engagement and marriage the more and more I think men are getting the raw end of the deal. Why is it that men have to spend thousands of dollars on a ring to propose with? In a way, this is like purchasing a wife. It sounds bad, but you can't really propose without a ring. So until you save up money to buy the ring....you have no wife. Do you see what I am saying?
In today's society where women and men are suppose to be equal in all things....why not the engagement? Here is my idea. LET THIS BE WRITTEN: From now on, if a woman wants to marry a man, they have to present them with a plasma T.V. It seems like a fair trade. A plasma costs about the same as a ring, sometimes cheaper. This way both the bride and the groom enter into the marriage equally. What do you think?

Cleaning Up Christmas

Now that Christmas is over, it is time to start cleaning up. My least favorite part of the cleanup is taking down the tree. We use an artificial tree in our house, which makes the clean up a pain in the neck. Why don't they make the boxes that the tree comes in a little bigger? Why must it be jammed packed into the box in the first place? I know that this saves space, but come on! Every year when the time comes we have to try and shove the tree back into the box. This usually consists of having someone sit on the box while I try and wrap duct tape around it (looks like a weird game of twister), branches are poking through the corners and ripping the box up. Maybe I am the only one that has problems like this?

2 Sneezing Myths

1. I had always heard that getting pepper in your nose would make you sneeze. FALSE. Contrary to what you see in Bugs Bunny cartoons, this doesn't work. I personally snorted some pepper yesterday and nothing happened. A little burning maybe, but no sneeze.

2. Another sneezing myth that I have busted. So called experts have always said you can't sneeze and keep your eyes open. If you did your eyes would pop out due to the 100 mph of force from the sneeze. FALSE. Just 2 hours ago I was able to sneeze and keep my left eye open. Although it did hurt a little bit, my eye definitely did not pop out.

Death by Water

My wife is a nurse, so she is always talking about strange medical things. The other day she was trying to tell me that you could die from drinking too much water. I found the thought of this crazy! I know you can drown from water and that's it. How else could water kill you? Water is our friend; we depend on it to live. So after betting her a million dollars she was wrong, I decided to "Google" it. What I found out was astonishing. For the first time in my life, I was wrong!
Drinking too much water can kill you. Here's the scoop:
"Water intoxication (also known as hyperhydration or water poisoning) is a potentially fatal disturbance in brain function that results when the normal balance of electrolytes in the body is pushed outside of safe limits by a very rapid intake of water."
To put in it Brogan terms..... WATER KILLS! So beware. Next time you crack open that bottled water, just know this....IT COULD KILL YOU!

Rocky Mountain Oysters

What is the origin of Rocky Mountain Oysters? This is one of life's biggest mysteries. I asked around and this is the explanation that I found out.

What are Rocky Mountain oysters? They are that part of the male cow that is removed in his youth so that he may thereby be more tractable, grow meatier, and behave less masculine. When the calves are branded, the testicles are cut off and thrown in a bucket of water. They are then peeled, washed, rolled in flour and pepper, and fried in a pan. They are considered to be quite a delicacy. Like other organ meats, testicles may be cooked in a variety of ways – deep-fried whole, cut into broad, thin slices, or marinated. At roundups in the old West, cowboys and ranch hands tossed the meat on a hot iron stove. When the calf fries exploded, they were done?

Eating animal genitalia dates back to ancient Roman times, when it was believed that eating a healthy animal's organ might correct some ailment in the corresponding human organ of the male person eating it. Because of this belief, the practice continues to the present day, especially in Asia, where animal genitalia are considered an aphrodisiac.

The rugged folks of the Rocky Mountain region are not squeamish. Testicle festivals are held every spring and fall in Montana. These festivals can be very rowdy and may not be the best place to bring your children. If you can't get to a festival, many restaurants and bars in Montana, Idaho, and Kansas serve Rocky Mountain oysters all year long and with less fanfare.

Bathroom Bars

I don't know about you, but when I drink alcohol I have to urinate every five minutes. I am being serious. It almost takes the fun out of drinking. If I am at a crowded bar and have been drinking quite a bit you will never see me.....Unless you are in line with me for the bathroom. The worst case scenario is when a really busy drinking establishment has a single bathroom. I try to avoid these places at all costs. But of course after a few drinks and that urge to urinate is too much, I sometimes get creative (just another example of something that only alcohol can make you do). The beauty of being a man is we can go to the bathroom just about anywhere.

Why does Asparagus Make My Urine Smell?

This is an old age question that needs to be answered. Why is it, that every time I eat asparagus my urine smells really weird? Finally I took the time to look it up, and here is what I found. I hope you feel enlightened.

"Asparagus contains a sulfur compound called mercaptan. (It's also found in rotten eggs, onions, garlic, and in the secretions of skunks.) When your digestive tract breaks down this substance, by-products are released that cause the funny scent. The process is so quick that your urine can develop the distinctive smell within 15 to 30minutes of eating asparagus.

While eating asparagus may make your urine smell strange, it won't harm you. Actually, asparagus -- a member of the lily family along with garlic, onions, and leeks -- is a powerhouse of nutrients. It's an excellent source of folic acid (a B vitamin that may help protect against birth defects, heart disease, and cancer), a significant source of vitamin C (an antioxidant that may protect tissues against damage), and a good source of vitamin A (an antioxidant). Not to mention that asparagus contains 3 grams of fiber per 3.5-ounce serving and a host of health-enhancing plant chemicals, or phytonutrients, that may protect against disease.

Napkins

Where would the world be without napkins? Just think of the messy hands that there would be. You really don't appreciate a napkin until you don't have one. You get your favorite hamburger from a fast food place and drive off ready to enjoy your tasty treat. Then you notice........no napkin. It doesn't seem like that big of deal at the time so you open up your juicy burger. After just the first bite, ketchup gets all over your hands. What do you do? Oh yes, the classic lick your fingers move comes into effect. It works, but then your hands are still wet.
Another one of my favorite napkin substitutes are socks. Oh come on, we all have done this. The logic behind using the socks in my mind is if you have pants on nobody is going to see any mustard stains on your socks. It is better then wiping it on your car seat. Plus, socks are easier to wash.

Shoe Talk

Why do we go to such great lengths to break in a new pair of shoes? I just bought a new pair of shoes that really hurt my feet. But, I keep thinking that they will eventually "break in". I figure the more I wear them the more they will conform to my feet. But as the days go by, my feet keep hurting more and more. Maybe my feet are "breaking in" and not my shoes?

I think the most extreme example of this for me is when I bought new sandals for my cruise 4 years ago. They were probably the coolest sandals that I have ever seen in my 28 years on this earth. I spent quite a bit of money on them (for me it was a lot, I am kind of cheap) and was hell bent on wearing them the entire vacation. The sandals were fine for walking around the cruise ship, a little uncomfortable, but not bad. The next day the boat docked in the Bahamas. I had booked a trip to a private island for snorkeling and a grill out. It sounded perfect! Little did I know that I would have to walk over 3 miles to get to the boat to take me to the private island. This is when my sandals decided to act up a bit. Underneath the buckle on the side, the metal began to dig into my skin. A blister formed... then blood began to trickle down my foot. I was in horrible pain...... So I finally made it to the island and let me tell you, the salt water felt so great on the new cuts on my feet (ouch). When my time on the island was over, I had to make the painful walk back to the cruise ship. I swore at that point I would never wear those sandals again..... The next day rolled around and I thought I would give the sandals one more try. By now they had to have been "broken in", right? Besides, I paid so much money, I couldn't just let them go to waste. WRONG! I slipped the sandals on and the metal buckle immediately pierced back into my open wound. I screamed like a little girl. I took the sandals off and ran to the top deck of the ship. I ran to the edge and launched the sandals overboard into the sea. I raised my arms in victory and belted out "I'm king of the world"! I felt so free.

Did I learn my lesson? Apparently not. I sit hear typing this with my new shoes on, waiting for them to "break in". Sometimes I am an idiot.

Store Questions

I know people are just doing their jobs when they ask you questions at stores. Maybe they are just trying to be helpful. This is great, I appreciate it.....but if you work in a specialty store, this question is really not needed. The other day, this happened to me twice. First, I was at Blockbuster Video to rent a movie to watch. I was walking down the row of new releases and I heard a voice from behind me, "Is there anything I can help you find?" Well, since I am at a "movie store", I answered, "a movie". Did the lady really have to ask me? Just let me look at the movies and if I have a question I can find you.
The second example is my favorite. I am Irish, proud of it, and like to buy Irish products to show my heritage. I was at an Irish shop, that only sells Irish related products. I walked into the store.....and of course the lady working there had to ask the question....."Can I help you find anything?" So of course I answered "I am looking for something Irish, do you have anything?" Looking back on it, I should have been a complete smart butt and said, "I am looking for something German, do you have it?"

Both these examples go into the "Thanks, Captain Obvious" category. I know these workers are just trying to do there job, but I still get a kick out of it. I guess they could ask more specific questions, but we know they really don't care anyway.

A Catwalk in the Movie Theater

Now that most movie theaters have stadium seating I have noticed something. Since you walk in at the bottom of the seating rows everyone is watching you. It seems that the walkway in front of the movie screen has become a catwalk. I know that once I have found my seat and no previews are on I am watching the newbies that walk in. We check out their clothes, who they are with, make comments on their mullets and so forth and so on. We are also watching to see who will sit by us. For some reason I always get stuck next to an overweight person (not that there is anything wrong with that) that takes up way too much room and takes up my armrest. So when I see somebody that fits that description I am just praying that they don't sit next to me.
So why not put a catwalk or runway up there? I would love it if they put on some dance music and a spotlight as soon as I entered the theater. Then I could shake my little behind on the catwalk for all the onlookers to see and comment on.

Up In the Clouds

I recently traveled to Columbus, Ohio. On my flight there it caught my attention that there were a lot of people around me that prayed while on the airplane. It was snowing on my return flight and we ran into some turbulence. The plane was starting to feel more like a roller coaster ride (a shaky one like the Tornado). It is amazing how people all of a sudden find God when faced with danger in their life. On an ordinary day they would not even think about God in their life. But when a scary situation arrives......BAM!! They are asking God for help. Hmmmmm....
On a related note............ A thought on being a Christian and being an Atheist. A Christian really has nothing to lose by believing in God. If there is no God then the Christian is just crazy. On the other hand, an Atheist has much more to lose. If there is no God, then they were right. If they are wrong, and everything in the Bible is true, then they have much more to worry about.

NKNC Attitude

Only 145 days left until "Independant Thomas" is gone. Then the Wedding will be here. Don't get me wrong, I am very excited to take my vows with the woman I love. But lately I have seen some changes taking place in me. The one that worries me the most is my NKNC attitude. NKNC stands for "Not Knowing, Not Caring". This is my whole strategy towards my appearance.
I used to be considered borderline "Pretty Boy". I always had to have my hair looking perfect, had to be clean shaven and even had some Banana Republic outfits. Now I dress for Thunderdome. I just don't care. I don't know if it because I don't have to impress the ladies anymore or what. I will now go out in public without gel in my hair! I throw on whatever is the most comfortable to run to the supermarket. WHAT IS WRONG WITH ME! I never shave on the weekend. By the time Sunday comes I resemble Big Foot.
I wonder if this is part of becoming older or just the beginning of married life as I know it? I guess as long as don't ever get matching jogging suits. That is where I must draw a line!

A Leap of Faith

Skydiving in my mind is just plain crazy. Would I like to do it? Yes. Would I actually do it? Probably not. It makes me wonder how the idea of skydiving came about. Who were these early adventurers? Was the first time just an accident gone bad? Or was it someone trying to commit suicide by jumping out of a plane that inspired the early skydivers. I can see the logic of that. You are standing there watching someone fall hundreds of miles to their death and you think, "Hey that looks like fun!"

The so called experts say it is safe because the first time you can do a tandem jump with an experienced skydiver. So instead of dying alone, at least you could die with someone else. Hmmmmmm. At least if I was going to do a tandem jump, I would want to jump with a woman. Because if something did go wrong and we fell to our death, I wouldn't want my last experience on Earth to be, screaming with a man attached to my backside.

Limo

Limos just aren't what they use to be. Back in the day a limo was a sign of prestige. You would see a limo driving by and wonder what famous person was in there. I think a lot of it had to do with the dark tint. As a society, we are very nosey. We want to see why this person is being hidden.
Today's limos look somewhat similar but are different. There are a lot more varieties to choose from. There are the stretch limos with hot tubs and even pimped out limos with complete audio systems and DVD players. But now, pretty much anyone can afford to rent a limo. You see them used at weddings, funerals and proms. I think the proms have tarnished the image of the limo the most. Anytime you see a bunch of drunk kids hanging out the sunroof it doesn't exactly scream prestigious. The person I really feel sorry for is the driver. Can you imagine how much puke a limo driver has to deal with?

The Fat Tuesday Taxidermy Idea

"Taxidermy (Greek for "the arrangement of the skin") is the art of mounting or reproducing animals for display (e.g. as hunting trophies) or study."

I was talking with some people from work and the subject of a taxidermist came up. I had mentioned that when I die I want my body to be preserved in some manner so that I can still be seen around my house. I figured if I was stuffed, then my wife could mount me on the wall and still see me each day. This way I could be certain that she would never marry another man. Because what man would marry a woman who had a man mounted on her wall? Plus, could you really see "messing around" when your dead husband's eyes were watching you. Sure you could throw a shirt or pants over me, but I will still be there hanging out. That is just weird!

Wonder Drugs

So I was watching some television last night and I saw a very strange commercial. It was a commercial for a drug named Valtrex. If I would have had the television muted I would have thought it was for couples who had just won 10 million dollars or found out they are going to live forever. But no, Valtrex is a drug for people with Genital Herpes. If you don't know what genital herpes is here you go:

"Genital herpes is an STD that typically appears as one or more blisters on or around the genitals or rectum. The blisters break, leaving tender ulcers (sores) that may take two to four weeks to heal the first time they occur."

So back to the commercial. The couples they show on this commercial are riding bikes, taking hikes, hugging each other, jumping for joy and acting like life is perfect. DID YOU SEE THE DEFINITION ABOVE? I don't think the first thing I would do if I had a blister on my rectum is to jump on a bike and take a ride around town. These drug commercials don't make any sense. Valtrex may help with certain symptoms, but don't sugar coat the truth. If you lead people to think that STDs aren't that bad for you, and can be controlled with a drug, then they will think, why have safe sex? This means more and more STDs will be passed around.

Date Food

Going on a first date can be a very intimidating situation, especially if it is a blind date. One thing that I have learned is that if you go out to eat, what you order can really make a difference. My first advice is to never order a salad. A salad is just too much of a risk. You could get dressing on your clothes because the lettuce doesn't always cooperate. If you do choose a salad don't choose cheese sticks for an appetizer. I have been preaching this for years. When you eat the cheese sticks, the cheese goes straight to the bottom of your stomach and begins to plug it up. Then when you eat the lettuce on top of that, it has no where to go. So the lettuce is exposed to your warm stomach acid and wilts. This creates some obvious stomach concerns. Nobody wants to have to do their "duty" on a date!
Next comes choosing an entrée. The worst thing you could order on a first date is spaghetti or any other pasta. We all know eating pasta can get a little messy. You don't want to be sucking up noodles in front of your date....It is not attractive. Plus, you could get sauce all over your clothes. One last bit of advice about choosing an entrée. Stay away from food with a lot of garlic or onion, especially if you didn't come prepared with a breath mint or gum. Nobody likes "dragon breath".

The Drinking Fountain Incident

I did it. I never thought I would, but it happened. I tried to be strong, I tried to hold out........ But I couldn't! I am ashamed of myself. I cheated on my girl spouse...... with a drinking fountain.
I have no excuses..... Yes I was thirsty..... Yes I had a sore throat. But still I should have just walked away. It was so shiny and polished. It was calling out to me! I couldn't control myself. I made my move..... I slowly and gently pushed the button on the fountain. I got an uneasy feeling in my stomach in anticipation for the water. As the water begin to flow I noticed something was wrong. The water was only coming out of the spout a few centimeters. I tried to push the button harder, hoping to get some more water to flow out.... Nothing happened. What was I suppose to do? I had gone this far already. But, I didn't want to put my mouth where thousands of other germ harvesting mouths had been. I was in too deep. I couldn't stop myself. I lowered my head and took the dive....... Then it hit me. I just made out with a water fountain!

Chicken Pot Pie

Have you ever wondered what was in your chicken pot pie?
After you get done tasting that first bite you wonder why?

Why would you eat something that looked the way it did?
Tastes like chicken and onion, but looks like squid!

Once when I was eating a chicken pot pie it began to wiggle.
Then I freaked out when it talked and started to giggle.

I poked the pie with my mighty fork,
I hit something, a piece of pork?

I ran to the garbage and threw it away with a sigh,
Still not knowing what was in my chicken pot pie

Free Beer at the Mall

Well, not really free, but deserved. What am I talking about? You know in the middle of malls they have seating areas that are usually taken up by men waiting for their wives to charge up the credit card. I have this great new idea on how to improve these stomping grounds for bored men. First of all you need to enclose the area with walls. Next there needs to be plasma televisions lining the walls showing sports games or manly action movies. Sounds good already doesn't it? Here is what takes it to the next level. Each man as they walk in is given a little handheld PDA. Each time their wife or significant other spends some money it tallies up on the screen. For every $50.00 spent, the man gets a free beer. So really this works out for the man and the woman. They are both happy! Heck after a few beers, some husbands might even agree to the buy that blue Coach purse their wife wants.

At the Right Place, Wrong Time

Does this ever happen to you? You are walking out of a room into a hallway and you almost run into another person. Not only did you almost run into them, but you are heading in the same direction. This always happens to me! Now the fun begins. It is not that bad if the other person is a speed walker. Then there are no problems at all. They get ahead of you and are out of sight in no time at all. The problem people are those that walk at the same pace as you. You don't really want to talk to this person, but you end up walking right next to them for what seems to be an eternity. This just seems awkward. Usually what happens is that one person tries to speed up so that you aren't walking right next to each other. But sometimes both of you will try and speed up and end up on the same pace again. So then you try and slow down so that the other person can get ahead of you. All this work and you were just trying to walk across the building!

This is similar to when you get behind a group of people who are walking very slowly. The problem is that they don't allow the space to get around them. These people are usually talking to each other and paying no attention to the world around them. So you look for a time to pass. Suddenly you feel like Jeff Gordon trying to find a lane to pass. You have to slow your pace down and just wait… Then suddenly you see your opportunity and you have to do that speed walk to make it by. You know the walk where you are almost running, pumping your arms in desperation in an attempt to get that extra boost.

Some Bling for your Belly

Much like champagne, Goldschlager has a reputation as a celebration drink. It is touted by style consultants for its ability to increase one's inner bling. Goldschlager actually has little flakes of gold floating around in it. For those of you who don't know, Goldschlager is hard liquor that has a cinnamon taste. So one night my friend and I were drinking some Goldschlager with some Bailey's Irish Crème (Oatmeal Cookie). After a few drinks I noticed that both full bottles were gone. This is when things started to get interesting. My friend began to feel sick to her stomach. She stumbled and fell to the ground. She then proceeded to vomit all over the wall. By this time I was feeling a little gross myself and went to bed. The next morning I woke up and noticed that something shiny was on the wall. The gold flakes had stayed stuck on the wall where the vomit was. Wow. I now had a gold wall. It just goes to show, drinking does pay off sometimes!

In the Elevator

I am so uncomfortable in elevators with other people. I don't know why. There is just something about being confined to a small area with a stranger that just makes my skin crawl. You notice how there is always an awkward silence that is happening. Occasionally you will get the person who tries to break the silence by making a comment on the weather. Otherwise there is just plain, uneasy silence.

I guess the whole elevator riding experience is determined by who you are with. As we all know, most elevators don't have the best ventilation system. This could make for a very bad ride. There is sometimes the lady with too much perfume or even worse the man with way too much cheap aftershave. The sweet smell just makes you sick to your stomach and seems to stick to your clothing. You do everything you can to hold your breath and just pray that the elevator door will open soon. I have even gotten off an elevator before my stop due to some smells (bad gas).

I also notice that I am always looking up at the numbers. I try not to make direct eye contact with the other person in the elevator. I notice a lot of other people use this technique as well. I just pray that I never get stuck in an elevator. I think I might be scarred for life!

The Mental Mirror

Sometimes I can look in the mirror and think that I am the hottest guy on the planet. Other times I can't stand the look of my ugly, Shrek like face. It is amazing how our mood and self-esteem can change the way we think about ourselves. Have you ever heard the expression "mind over matter"? This is so true of our lives as humans.

With the recent craze of plastic surgery in our society, it makes me wonder what I would change about myself. Other than the obvious, butt implants, I think I like the cards that I was dealt in the looks department. Would you change anything about yourself? Would it take the scalpel of a doctor or can a change in the way you think about yourself do the trick? My thoughts.....Positive thinking is free.

The Colgate Curse

If you are like me, you brush your teeth two times a day or maybe even more. The "Colgate Curse" applies to the morning brush. This is the brush before you are exposed to the world, and nobody wants to introduce Mr. Morningbreath to everyone. Keep in mind, this may only happen to me, so I need your feedback......
So there I am, finishing up brushing, spitting out that last mouthful of water and then wiping off my face of any excess toothpaste. I look in the mirror and I think to myself, "There is one good-looking guy, with some minty fresh breath to say the least". But, I have made a fatal error... I have forgotten about......"THE COLGATE CURSE". It usually doesn't hit you until an hour later. You are sitting at work and notice a white paste on your pants.

What is that? That has to be toothpaste. Right?! What was I doing last in these pants? Hmmm.. Then you try to take some water and rub out the white stain.... IT ONLY MAKES IT WORSE. Now the stain has spread out even more. What will others think? AHHHHH, "The Colgate Curse" has gotten me again! Did I make you look at your pants for that white stain?

The Moving Stairs

Sometimes right before I get on an escalator I get a little nervous. I am always paranoid that my footing will be off and I will fall flat on my face. In my 28 years on this Earth has it happened? No. Which means the odds are against me.

Why do they need that emergency stop button? I remember being told of horror stories when I was little about somebody's clothes getting caught in the moving stairs and them being sucked under and killed. That can't be true...Can it?

I think my paranoia is a good thing. Better safe than sorry. One thing I know for certain.... I will always tie my shoe laces before getting on an escalator!

A Bozo Nightmare

I am afraid of clowns. No I am not joking. I can't stand to be around them or even look at them. The kid friendly character is a nightmare to me. I still wake up sometimes in the middle of the night, in a puddle of sweat because I have a dream about waking up in bed and seeing a clown standing at the foot of my bed. If I saw Bozo the clown I would run in fear!

So what is this fear?

"Coulrophobia is the fear of clowns. In discussions of causes of coulrophobia, sufferers seem to agree that the most fear-inducing aspect of clowns is the heavy makeup, often accompanied by the bulbous nose and weird color of hair that conceals the wearer's identity."

I really think this stems back to 3 things in my childhood:

1. The Movie "IT" (Stephen King)

2. The Movie "Killer Clowns from Outerspace"

3. A TV show I saw about John Wayne Gacy, an American serial killer. He was convicted of murder of 33 boys and men, 27 of whom he buried in a crawl space under the floor of his house, while others were found in nearby rivers. He became notorious as the "Killer Clown" because of the many block parties he attended, entertaining children in a clown suit and makeup, under the name of Pogo the Clown.

I dare you to watch these shows and not have a fear of the clown. These shows are just plain messed up! I am think I need to start a support group and get some help.

Sweaters Anonymous

It is freezing outside today. The average temperature the last 5 days has been 1 degree. Now that is what I call cold my friends. But for some strange reason, I still manage to sweat. Now, I have always had a sweating problem. I blame genetics for the one flaw in an otherwise perfect body (puke now). It seems like everyone in my family sweats a lot. So this is nothing new. But today as I drove to work I stopped to think about it. Why do I sweat when it is so cold out? I get into the car with a long sleeved shirt and my winter coat on, (If I didn't, I would die of hypothermia) and begin my drive to work. Every morning, the same thing... I "pit out". It's a no win situation. Either I freeze to death or I go to work "pitted out". Life choices are so hard. Does this happen to anybody else out there?

Hair You Go

I was starving! I hadn't eaten in 9 hours. I sat down and ordered a plate of my favorite food, chicken fingers. Plus, the restaurant I was eating at had the best buttermilk ranch to dip the tasty fingers in. I was excited and felt myself salivating. I remember remarking to my dinner partner, "I am so hungry, I could eat a horse." Which, if you think about it, is a very stupid saying. I really wouldn't eat a horse. But that is neither here nor there. Back to the story... The server brought out my chicken fingers and I started to dive in. Just as I dipped my first finger into the creamy ranch dressing I spotted it. No, it can't be.... Is that.... GROSS! There was a hair on my plate. Not just any hair, but a long, black, curly hair. I had to force myself not to throw up in my mouth. I had totally lost my appetite. I ended up sending my food back. Sure, I got my money back, but my appetite was gone. Isn't it amazing how one little hair can totally ruin a great dinner? That is the power of the mind!

Health Insurance

Last week I received a medical guide from my health care insurance provider. The guide shows different medical conditions and symptoms that affect the human body. Now, why would my health insurance provider send this to me? Is this so I can diagnose my own conditions and not visit the doctor? Or is it to make me so paranoid about having certain conditions that I would go to the doctor? I would assume that my health insurance provider wants me to be in great physical and mental health and generally care about my well being. But, after reading a few chapters in the medical guide, I think that they are just plain messing with my mind.

I feel that I am in pretty good health. Granted, I may not be able to walk upstairs in my house without running out of breath, but I get along. After reading the guide, I noticed that I had several of the symptoms for many of the medical conditions in the book. The more I read, the more I began to panic. Could I have Jondus, Avian Flu or Athlete's foot?..... My ear hurts.... What does this mean? My left pinky finger has a bump on it! What should I do?

So I visited the doctor after I calmed down. I found out that I really wasn't going through menopause or that I really didn't have Athlete's Foot. But, I did find out something that others have been saying for years.... I am crazy, thanks in part to my health insurance provider.

The Wet Touch

I had just washed my hands after using the restroom at my office. I somewhat dried my hands and began my exit out the door. Just then I heard someone from behind me call out my name. I turned around and saw an old acquaintance who I hadn't seen for a number of years. He went to shake my hand and I froze. My hands were still a little wet from the bathroom. I can't shake his hand with a wet hand. That is just awkward. He might think that I just urinated on my hand. I know how gross it is when I have to shake somebody's hand that is wet. It's just gross! I didn't have time to think of any excuses for being rude, so I just hugged him. This was completely weird, for both of us. I don't think he knew what to do. I ended the embrace..... Complete silence. Then he just walked away. Wow! That went well. He may think that I am a little weird, but at least he didn't think I had urine on my hand!

The One Dollar Pregnancy Test

As I have mentioned many times, I am a cheapskate. So it makes sense that I like the Dollar Store. So I was strolling through my local Dollar Store (the one where everything is actually a dollar) getting in line for the checkout when I noticed a pregnancy test for a $1.00. What!? It was just sitting there as an impulse buy item with candy and gum. A few things came to my head when I saw this. First, who just thinks at the last minute they need a pregnancy test and just picks one up as an impulse buy? Second, can you really trust the results from a pregnancy test that costs a $1.00? I mean, come on. Having a child is a pretty big event in your life. Shouldn't you at least shell out $10.00 or more for a name brand one? What's next?....... a one dollar rock climbing rope? Don't know if I would trust that one

Kissing Santa Claus

I wonder if the kid who saw "momma kissing Santa Claus" is messed up for life. He not only saw the kiss, but he stayed there to see "momma tickle Santa Clause" too. It is kind of a perverted song if you think about it. Not really what Christmas is supposed to be about.

Tossing the Cookies

Well, I puked this past weekend for the first time in 3 years. I forgot how much I loved to puke! I can't think of anything that tastes as bad as puke. There is just something unpleasant about the combination of warm bile and mucus that isn't that appealing.

But, one time when I was little, I remember puke actually tasting good. I know, that sounds crazy. But, when I was little and had the flu, my parents would have me eat jello. On one particular occasion I was eating lime green jello (one of my favorites). I remember eating an entire bowl of the tasty green jello just a couple of hours after I had first puked. By this time I was feeling somewhat better and I ate the jello like it was going out of style...... Three minutes later I went running to the bathroom trash container to heave up the green liquid. I bent over the trash can and the green jello came spewing out. After my final heave, I could taste the limey green goodness of the jello on my lips. I remember thinking to myself, "Wow, that doesn't taste bad."

Moral of the Story: For a pleasant puking experience, try Lime Green Jello (that should be a commercial).

Drinking Wine in Bed

I get a kick out of the mattress commercials I see on television. The mattress company tries to impress us by showing how you can set a glass of red wine on one side of the bed and then lay down on the other side without the wine spilling. Now, I am not a raging alcoholic, so I might not know for sure. But, how many people are drinking wine in bed and then need to set the glass down on their bed. Have they ever heard of a night stand?
Then you have the commercial with the bowling ball being dropped on the mattress. This makes sense. Just the other day I was bowling in bed and it kept my wife up all night.
I know these commercials are just trying to prove a point with the wine and bowling ball, but why not show us something that shows the mattress working for a practical use? You could show a fat man (or woman), jumping into bed after their spouse is already asleep. With a normal mattress, the fat man sends his spouse flying out of bed. With the new improved mattress, the spouse doesn't lose one second of sleep!

Memoirs of a Straw

I was eating dinner at one of my favorite local restaurants. I had a wonderful fried walleye sandwich and some tasty waffle fries to eat in front of me. To drink, I had some ice cold Cherry Pepsi Soda (Yes, its soda). In my mind, there is no better way to drink a soda then with a straw. Which most of the time is no big deal. But once in a while I seem to loose all hand eye coordination with the process of drinking from a straw. This was one of those times.

So I went to grab my half full glass (gotta think positive) of soda. As I was bringing the glass towards my mouth the straw went straight into my nose. OOOPS! (Now I realize I have a big nose, but this just shouldn't happen.) My cat-like reflexes snatched the straw out of my nose. My first thought was.... Did anybody see? I paused to look around to see if anybody was laughing. I think I made it. I was in the clear. Now, should I drink from the straw even though it was in my nose? If I didn't drink from the straw again it would appear strange. So, to save face I stuck the snot infested straw in my mouth and took up a slurp of soda.

Another Ring tone Bites the Dust

I should have learned my lesson a long time ago.... But I didn't. Another song has been ruined because of my cell phone. It always sounds like a good idea to have a song you like as your ring tone on your phone.... But it isn't. After a week or so of hearing a 15 second rendition of your favorite song 10-15 times a day you start to really hate the song. It even gets annoying. It gets to the point where you hear it on the radio and it feels like you are taking crazy pills! You have been warned.

Stolen Identity

The other day I was driving to work and noticed something out of place. A Honda Civic passed me by and it has a Lexus emblem on the back. Now, I have owned both a Lexus (see picture below of what happened to my old Lexus) and a Honda, so I know what they look like. How stupid does this guy think we are? I understand trying to impress your friends and girls, but this just makes you look stupid. Ripping off a Honda logo and slapping on a $10.00 Lexus emblem doesn't make your car cool. It makes you look like the village idiot. One other thing about this car that really annoyed me was it had a special muffler to let you know that it was coming from a mile away. What's the point? To me it sounds more like you need to take your car to the shop than something that impresses people. I guess whatever floats your boat.

A New Perspective

Last night I bought a black light to look for some pet stains (you can also see blood, urine, semen, puke and much more) around my house and was taken into a different dimension all together! When the lights went out and the black light turned on I was welcomed to a world of stains, lint and who knows what else. It was horrible. I almost began to have a panic attack!

I consider myself to be a clean person. But after looking at my house under the black light, I am afraid to walk around without socks on. It is amazing how much the human eye doesn't pick up under normal light. Once the lights came back on and the black light went off, my life was back to normal. It was like a bad dream.

Avoiding Capture

I don't understand the radar detector. I know what they are for... I am not that stupid. But, I don't understand why people think that they can speed without getting caught. It seems rather obvious to me, that if you own a radar detector that you must speed. Why else would you have it? (Unless you are abnormally paranoid from smoking up) If I was a police officer and saw a driver with the detector hanging on the window I would follow them around until they started speeding. Plus, have you driven with somebody who has a radar detector thru town? The stupid device goes off all the time. Automatic doors set it off. So how accurate can these devices be? I think I will save my $200 and just drive the speed limit (5 miles over).

Melba Toast & Croutons

If there is no date on my box of Melba Toast, then how can I tell when it is old? I mean it's already hard as a rock.

On a related note.... Do you like old bread? Well if you love croutons, then you love old bread. Did you know that most restaurants use old stale bread to make their croutons from? Yep, they just cut the old bread into cubes, add some oil, seasonings and then bake.

Wizard Showdown

Who would win in a battle between Dumbledore (wizard from Harry Potter movies) and Gandalf (wizard from Lord of the Rings)? They are both pretty old and scrappy looking. My money would be on Dumbledore. He seems like he wouldn't mind fighting dirty and sometimes to take out a fellow wizard you need to hit below the belt. What do you think?

I Have the Power

Do you ever walk under a street lamp and it turns off or on the moment you cross under it? This seems to happen to me a little too often. I have come to the conclusion that I have some kind of bioenergy field around me that affects electricity. I am not joking! This is not more of Brogan's Blarney. I think I have a gift.................. As I was typing this my computer screen flickered on and off. Was that power outage during last month's storm due to weather?........ or maybe it was just my powers in effect. Hmmmmm.......

Crumbs in the Silverware Drawer

I just don't understand it. I put my silverware in the dishwasher and turn it on. Once it is finished I open it up and I have shiny, sparkling silverware. I carry my silverware over to the designated drawer and place them in their slot. So, to my knowledge, the silverware is clean. But somehow, the next time I open up the drawer full of clean silverware there are crumbs in the silverware tray......... Why? How can it be? Are there crumb gnomes that come and sprinkle the crumbs in there when I am gone? This has to be one of life's great mysteries.

Play On Words

Sometimes it's weird for me to hear a woman refer to her friend as a "girlfriend". But, it seems socially accepted for women to say this. On the other hand, if I told somebody that I was going to play basketball with my "boyfriend" it might sound a little odd and confusing. It could be interpreted that I was gay (not that there is anything wrong with that) because I referred to my friend who happens to be a boy, and my friend, as "boyfriend". It's funny the way that works. Something as little as the way we refer to another person can define who we are in another person's eyes.

Pizza Delivery & Cops

Is there some sort of unwritten law, or a real law for that matter, that the public knows nothing about, that allows pizza delivery drivers to speed? Because I have to tell you I have noticed many cars with the pizza sign on them buzz past me doing at least 90mph on a 25mph street. Now granted I may not be the fastest driver in the world (my wife will tell you I drive like a grandpa), but come on! I never see those pizza cars pulled over. Do you? I think that the police department is getting some free pizza out of this deal. We make fun of cops for always wanting donuts, but the truth is that pizza is the number one addiction for them. This addiction allows 16 year old kids to cruise around town driving like maniacs in their old Dodge Neon with a pizza sign lit up on top. I mean come on. The light on top of the car even draws attention to the speeding cars and they still don't get pulled over. I challenge somebody to test my theory. Get a hold of one of these pizza signs and drive around town like a crazy person. Speed, hit garbage cans, run red lights, see if you get pulled over. My prediction..............you won't. And no I won't pay for your ticket if you get one.

Good Old Name Tags

Does any body actually enjoy wearing name tags? For some reason I always feel stupid when I wear one.... Somebody walks up to me stares down at my tag and says "Hi, Thomas", even though they have no clue who I am. Maybe, I am just anti-social? Maybe I should embrace the name tag idea and take it one step further. I know what I will do... I am going to buy 7 t-shirts with THOMAS spelled out (in bold hot pink print) on them and wear a different one each day of the week. That way everybody knows my name.

No Cash

I never carry cash any more. I just pay with my debit card for all my purchases. This makes life so much easier and you don't have to handle paper money with all of its germs. I don't understand why people can't accept this? What do I mean? Well during the holidays when I go to the super market I have to walk by the Shriners or Knights of Columbus or Girl Scouts or some group of people who want a piece of my hard earned paycheck. I do realize that this money is going for a good cause (in some cases) and hell who wouldn't want to pay $10 for a tootsie roll, but I just don't have any cash to give these folks. I know what they are thinking when I say I don't have any cash. They are thinking that I am a cheap, selfish or just a bold-faced liar. But come on people, get with the times. Replace those rugged old red buckets with a debit card swipe. Then I would happily give you a few dollars!

Note to possible muggers: As you read above I don't carry cash (hint, hint, not worth your time)

Butt Marketing

I appreciate a good marketing idea. With that being said, what the heck is going on with messages on butts around the country? Do you know what I mean? You see sweatpants or jeans with little sayings like "Hottie", "Little Angel" or even "Bite Me" plastered right on the butt. It's bad enough that they make these pants for women. But they also have these for little girls. That is just messed up! What kind of pedophile thought of this idea? I would never buy my daughter a pair of these pants. What parent would want their child's butt being looked at by some old pervert? This is just another example of how this society is in a downward spiral.

The Joy of Nature

It was a wonderful crisp November evening tonight. I was outside on my deck grilling out some burgers when I took a moment to embrace the beautiful evening in front of me. The sun was setting, the moon was already showing it's glow and a flock of Canadian geese were flying down into the pond in my backyard. Amazingly, the first thing that came to my mind was taking a shotgun and shooting down one of the unsuspecting geese. I pictured myself in a real life "Duck Hunt" (Old Nintendo video game for you young folks), just picking the ducks off left and right. What a nice night.

Rachel Ray Thoughts

I would really love it if Rachel Ray made a dish that she didn't like. Every time I see her try one of her dishes, she acts as if it is better than sex. Of course she will throw in her catch phrase "Yum-O" quite a bit too, which can get very annoying. What I want to see is.... Rachel take a bit, spit out the food is disgust and shout out a few curse words. That would make my day.

My other thought on Rachel Ray is this....Those so-called "30 minute" meals take way longer than 30 minutes to make. Have you ever tried to make one? Not only does it take longer than 30 minutes but half the ingredients she uses to cook with I don't have on hand on a daily basis in my kitchen. So if you include running to the grocery store, it really is over an hour to make the meal if not more.

The Most Impersonal Christmas Gift

Holiday shopping is upon us once again this year. For some of us this can be a good thing, while for others it is just pure hell. I really think the person you are buying for makes the experience good or bad. I have some people who will give me a list of gift ideas as tall as me (6'1 if your counting). Then there are some others who won't even give me one inkling of an idea of what to buy them. These are the people who end up getting the gift card.

Now, I have always said that the gift card is the most impersonal gift. It doesn't really take any thought or effort on the buyer's part. But this year it has gotten even worse. Now you can order gift cards online. This means you don't even have to drive to the store to get the card. Better yet... you can have the gift card delivered directly to the person. You don't even have to see them! Isn't that great! Thanks to the modern convenience of the Internet you don't even have to deal with the family on Christmas anymore. You can send your gift card to them, send out an email instead of a card and spend you time on Christmas day at the one bar that is open in town. What has Christmas come to?

Smoker Dedication

I really have to hand it to smokers. They are so dedicated to their art. If I gave just 10 percent of their effort for smoking and used it towards working out I would look better than John Basedow (guy from annoying Fitness Made Simple commercials). Think about it............. Smokers know all the horrible medical effects of smoking, but yet they will still stand outside in below freezing temperatures to puff away. Cigarette prices go up, no problem.... they drive miles upon miles to another state to buy cartons (referring to the new Iowa tax). When bars and restaurants start to go smoke free nationwide I am sure they will find an answer. They have that hunger and the desire for that nicotine and nothing will stop them. It is amazing! I wish I could bottle that up and use it towards my goals. I will have to look into that.

A Trip to the Dentist

Two times a year it happens. I have 363 days a year of freedom. But, then I get that little postcard in the mail. It reminds me that my 6 month checkup at the dentist is near and I get that sick feeling to my stomach. I don't know why I fear the dentist so much. There is just something medieval about having metal objects jammed into your mouth that doesn't make sense to me. Every time I picture myself at the dentist it reminds me of a scene from the movie "Hostel" and I am part of some torture fantasy of a rich U.S. businessman. I guess the most ironic thing is I have to pay for this service (okay my insurance does, but still ironic).

So I am laying there with a spotlight in my face. A sharp metal object is picking at the layer between my gums and my teeth. I try to find a happy place and focus on counting the dots on the ceiling. But then, the dentist feels the need to add insult to injury. They begin to ask you questions. You know normal questions that a person would ask you at work or if you ran into an old friend at the market. You know like "How's the family doing?". Of course, all I can answer is "mmmmmmmmm", because I have something wedged between my #3 molar and #4 molar. So you really know that the person doesn't care what you have to say, when they know they won't get a coherent answer back from you.

So I put up with the 45 minutes of hell. The positive spin on this...... still no cavities. :)

You Say Kleenex, I Say Tissue

I hope you understand that Kleenex is a brand name. Not all tissues (a.k.a. snot rags) should be called Kleenex. So the next time you ask for something to blow your nose with make sure you ask for a "tissue".

Also, does anybody else ever have trouble getting that first tissue out of a new box? I always pull out 5 to star with. I can never get just one. Maybe it's because I am buying the cheaper brands and not Kleenex? So anywho, after that I always have a big wad of tissue that I just have to try and stuff into the box so it looks good. Life is so complex.

Thank God for My Key chain

Have you seen the key chains that you can buy with names on them? A lot of times you see them at gift stores and you buy them for your friends and family as a souvenir of someplace that they didn't get to visit. Really isn't that kind of rubbing in the fact that they are stuck at home? Okay that isn't here nor there. Anyways, I happen to have one of these key chains that say "Tom" on them. It may sound a little weird to carry around an item that has your name on it, but it comes in handy quite often. Just the other day I met somebody who I had never met before and during introductions I forgot my name. I panicked for a few seconds and then I remembered...... I pulled out my keys and there it was, "Tom". My name is Tom. Thank God for that key chain!

Road Trip Bathroom Break

When I am on a road trip and I need to tap a kidney (urinate), I usually pull off at a small town gas station. But for some reason I feel really guilty just making my deposit and leaving. I feel like I need to buy something from the station just in return for using their bathroom. I don't know why I feel this way? They offer their bathroom services free of charge, but you do get that "look", if you just walk in... and then walk out.... and I am not interested in pissing off a disgruntled, tired, underpaid gas station attendant who more than likely has a sawed off shotgun under the counter. So I usually try to find the cheapest thing I can, such as a piece of gum, purchase it and be on my way with a smile. I wonder if other people feel this way?

The Long Ride Home

Have you ever went and picked up your pizza instead of getting delivery? It is just plain torture! Usually when I end up ordering pizza I am to the point where I am starving. So I figure if I do carry-out I can save a few minutes (and a few buck on tips - I am cheap) and get the pizza a little quicker than with the delivery boy. But I don't think I can ever do that again. Once you get the hot, juicy, cheesy pizza in your car the torture begins. You can smell the aroma and the chemicals in your brain start going wild, you start salivating and little beads of sweat start falling in anticipation of your feast. This is one of those moments in life where you just want to go back to your savage caveman days and rip open that box and destroy that pizza. Another given is that on this journey home you will hit every red light known to man and get behind an 80 year doing 25mph on the highway. Yes, your 10 minute drive will feel like an eternity. So listen to my warning, go with delivery.

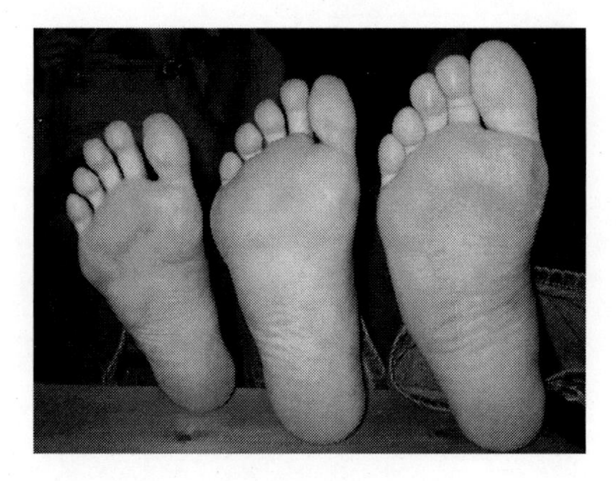

Feet

Feet are guides, the lead the way.
Giving support and taking no pay.

Sometimes feet really begin to stink and smell.
But, where you've been they will never tell.

The Bad Dining Smell

Have you ever gotten home from eating out and noticed your clothes smell horrible? This can really ruin a dining experience for me. Some restaurants just seem to leave the fried food smell lingering all over you. One place I have noticed it really bad is at the Mexican restaurant I eat at quite often. When I leave their I can't stand my own smell (I would rather smell like smoke). Don't get me wrong the food is excellent, but it makes me want to stop eating there. I just don't get it, some restaurants must have better ventilation. Moral of the story restaurant owners...... don't leave your patrons smelling like a fryer, spend that extra money on the best kitchen fan possible.

Black Tongue? Thanks Pepto-Bismol

Have you ever had an upset stomach and taken some Pepto-Bismol to take care of it? If so you may have been victim to the black tongue or poop caused by it. It can be scary if you know nothing about it. You wake up, look in your mirror and yikes!!!! Your tongue is covered in black and you may think you have a horrifying new disease. But relax it's only the Pepto. The reason why? Here's what I found out at the Pepto-Bismol website:

The active ingredient in Pepto-Bismol contains bismuth. When a small amount of bismuth combines with trace amounts of sulfur in your saliva and gastrointestinal tract, a black-colored substance (bismuth sulfide) is formed. This discoloration is temporary and harmless. It can last several days after you stop taking Pepto-Bismol.

Glitter Wrapping = Annoying

What's the deal with wrapping paper with glitter on it? It's just plain annoying! Apparently the makers of the wrapping paper used the least amount of glue as they could so that the glitter would end up everywhere but on the paper. When I get done unwrapping a present I end up looking like I am wearing glitter lotion or that I have just recently been to a strip club (if you have been to one you understand - try explaining that to your wife.... it was just a present. I swear!) Anyways, a note to anybody who ever decides to give me a gift. Just throw it in a gift bag or cash is great too, as long as it isn't in a card with confetti in it. That's a whole other headache.

The Past

Past the brush and through the hills, what will we find?

Past the outside of a person, what can we see?

Past the big words and political garbage, what is government?

Past, the time left behind, does anyone care?

Taken to the Cleaners

I normally don't take things to the cleaners very often. But, every so often I have to take my bed comforter to get cleaned because it is too large for my washer and dryer. As, I have mentioned numerous times in my blog, I am a cheapskate, so I usually go to whatever cleaners I have a coupon for. This time I ended up going to a place I had never been before. Anyways, I take in my comforter and drop it off. Two days later I go and pick up it up and pay the fee (which after the coupon was still $15.00. I get home and unwrap it and it smells horribly of cigarette smoke. Now, I don't smoke and it didn't go in smelling of smoke, so what the hell? I took the comforter there to clean it, hence the name cleaners, not get it smelling like an ashtray! So pretty much I paid $15.00 for nothing.... I was taken to the Cleaners, as the old saying goes. Needless to say, I won't be going there ever again.

Steven Siegel vs Jean-Claude Van Damme

Steven Siegel and Jean-Claude Van Damme have to be the worst two actors I have ever seen in a movie. But despite that fact, they keep making more and more movies. How is this possible? How can these no talent ass clowns keep getting paid to suck up the movie screen? I do have to admit that there is one Siegel movie that I do like. Executive Decision, a movie that came out in 1996 starring Halle Berry, is the one great Siegel movie. The reason..... He is only in it 5 minutes in the beginning and his character dies. It's great!

The only question worth asking about these two guys is who would win in a fight? The ponytail might give Siegel an edge, but I think Van Damme would come out on top. But who cares.... Chuck Norris could kick both of their butts.

High School Assumptions

Why do people assume that since I went to a certain high school that I know everyone who ever attended there? Whenever the subject ever comes up which high school I went to the person will say do you know "So and So" and 99 percent of the time I have no clue who they are talking about. They just assume that since there mother's, next door neighbor's, third child, who graduated 20 years before me and I went to school at the same place that we were best friends. Test out my theory. Tell someone you don't know very well where you went and see what happens. I can almost guarantee they will ask. Humans are so predictable.

Belly Button Theory

Does the world revolve around my belly button? Sometimes I feel that way, but generally I don't subscribe to this theory. What is the belly button theory? It states that you are the center of the universe and everything around you (and your belly button) is affected by your daily actions. Although.......

The last two times I needed to get gas I was driving home from work and each time I decided to wait until the next morning to fill up because I was too tired. The next morning on both occasions, gas went up over 15 cents a gallon. So the universe was punishing me for being lazy..... Gas prices went up because of little ol' me? Could this be? Maybe everyone should stop blaming George W.?.......Nah, It's gotta be his fault!

New Marriage Law

It seems to me that a lot of women cut their hair short after they get married. From what I have heard most men would rather their wives not do this. But, as husbands, who are we to say what our wives should do with their hair? So instead of trying to convince your wife to not chop off the hair you have grown to love here is what I suggest:

If your wife cuts her hair short, then you grow your hair out long. Yes, really long! First you will go thru that mullet period on your way to full out 80's rock star hair.... and if you are feeling really saucy, you can slick the long hair back with some gel and put it into a ponytail.

If all husbands united around the world to do this, women may think twice about cutting their hair after marriage.

Business Cards

I have been given hundreds of business cards over the years and only two or three of them have managed to escape a trip to my trash basket. What is the big deal about business cards? As soon as you meet someone new they slip one over to you. I think the card makes the person feel important to some extent. Yes, I have business cards myself, but the main thing I use them for is drawings to win prizes. You know what I'm talking about, don't you? A lot of businesses will keep that fish bowl on their counter to throw your business card in and win a prize. I think that is the best use of the business card. I am surprised the "green" folks haven't tried to ban the business card, because really, it is just a waste of paper. That would be one thing I would agree with them about.

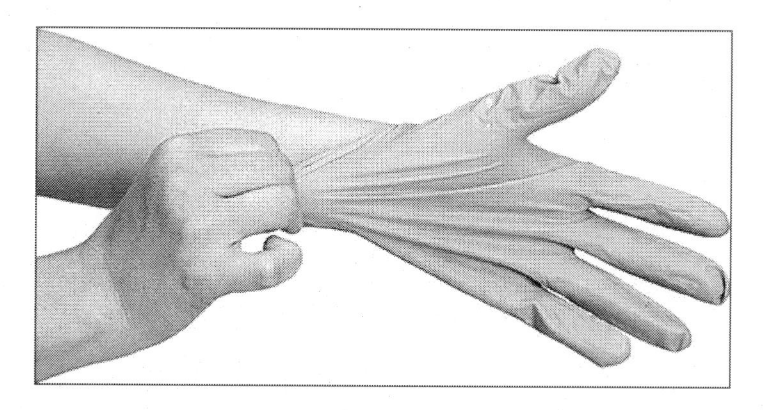

Latex Rubber Gloves Misunderstood

Rubber gloves + Anybody in the Room = A joke

That has been my observation when you put just about anybody in a room with a box of rubber gloves. They will slip the glove on and slap it up against their wrist like a doctor putting on one and will make some remark such as "Let me take a look in there". The strange part is that no matter how many times this has been used over the years as joke... people still laugh!

So does that make a Proctologist funny when he is giving you an exam? Well, if you are laughing during that, then I think maybe you might have other issues to worry about.

Fast Phone Message

I have been getting a lot of long-winded phone messages lately. I mean a couple of minutes worth of message. The bad thing is that when it gets to the end and the person leaves their phone number, they all of a sudden turn in to an auctioneer and belt out that number so fast I can't get it written down. You know what that means........... I have to listen to that whole message again to get the phone number. That does not make me happy camper.

What can we do to remedy this problem? Pass a law that you must leave your phone number twice at the end of a message. It's that easy. Problem solved.

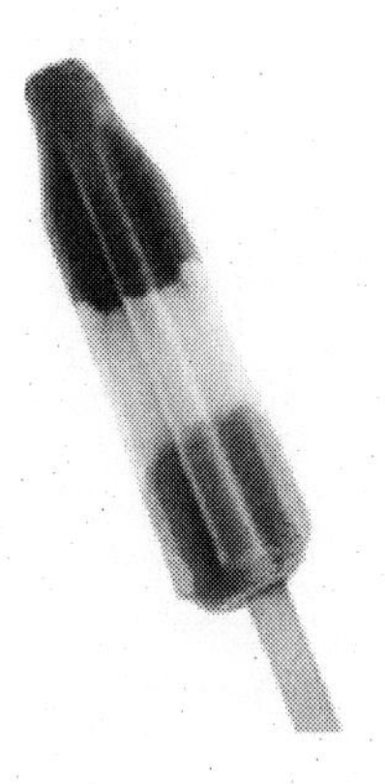

The Bomb Pop

I think that the white section of the Bomb Pop is my favorite. Since it doesn't have any artificial flavors it must be healthier for me too. After staring at the Bomb pop for a few minutes, I think they should have called it missile pop. Because when I think bomb I think more of a ball shape. This is more of a long missile shape (reminds me of something - I don't know what). And why is it Red, White and Blue? Is it saying that the U.S.A is known for bombs? So really the bomb pop is anti America? Hmmmmm. Maybe I shouldn't buy the bomb pop anymore? I will have to think about this one.

Cold Butter Blues

The bread at the beginning of a meal is one of my favorite parts of eating out. At most places you either get some butter to spread on it or oil to dip it in. The other day I was eating at a local restaurant, where they serve you butter with your bread. So we get our bread and I start getting excited. I rip off a piece and get ready to spread on my butter....... and that's where my bread bliss is over. The butter is cold and as hard as a rock! There is no way I can spread that out to all corners of my bread. Instead, I just place the little square block in the middle of my bread and try to spread it around. The result.... a torn up piece of bread with butter in the middle. I guess I just don't get it. I know that the people who run the restaurant have eaten out and had bread before. Don't they see that you must let the butter soften a little bit at room temperature before serving to their patrons? I know I sound a little picky, but it's these little things that make for a regular customer and a one timer.

Turning 30

Turning 30 can change your outlook on life. Does this mean life is over for me? Heck no, it's just the beginning. I have so much more to learn, many places to travel and I am going to be a dad. The sky is the limit you could say. Although I will admit by body doesn't recover from physical strain like it use to, all in all I feel good! So, by turning 30 do I have some wisdom I would like to pass on. Here is a list of 30 things I have learned in 30 years:

1. Never eat yellow snow.
2. What happens in Vegas stays in Vegas.
3. Liquor before beer, you're in the clear.
4. Don't order a burger at a place known for Pizza.
5. When somebody tells you a plate is hot, don't touch it.
6. Don't drink the water in Mexico.
7. Don't try and sniff pepper, it won't make you sneeze.
8. Yes, Pepto-Bismol does make your tongue turn black.
9. Rocky Mountain oysters......yeah they're not oysters.
10. Mayonnaise is so much better with fries than ketchup.
11. Sometimes a pen is mightier than a sword.
12. Chicken fingers.... a gift from God
13. Limos are way overrated.
14. Probably shouldn't bumper slide on the back of a truck.
15. Catnip is for cats only.
16. Wrestling is not real, just like Santa Claus
17. You really can never win playing slots.
18. Man was not meant to go down snowy hills at extreme speeds with two sticks on his feet.
19. A grease burn just plain hurts!
20. Never believe everything you read.
21. Always think before you talk.
22. Jumping over midgets in Mexico is illegal.
23. Never pick up a lit firework.
24. Never order a dish that means "Angry Dish"
25. When playing paint ball... always wear a cup.
26. God does work in mysterious ways.
27. Try not to puke in your brand new car. It's hard cleaning the yak out of the cracks.
28. When you get a chance to travel... go you may never get another chance.
29. My parents were right.
30. Put your pride to the side and try to be open minded to new things.

The Alarm Clock

There are some mornings when I wish I could just bash my alarm clock with a bat. I usually feel like this when I have had a really terrible night of sleep. The worst for me is when I have something really important going on the next morning. My internal alarm clock is off by a few hours. I will have my alarm set for 6:30am. I wake up at 4:30am on my own. Then starts the most miserable two hours of my day. I don't think I really get back to sleep after that. It is just a series of me looking over at the clock thinking that it is time to wake up. But, really when I am looking over only a matter of minutes have passed. I think this might be what hell is like.
Other mornings my alarm clock just doesn't go off at all. I forgot to set it, radio is turned down to low or my personal favorite, I set it for pm instead of am. This is one of the most paranoid feelings I can have in my day. I wake up feeling good (really because I got a few extra hours of sleep) and then I look over at the clock. I am 3 hours late to work! It is like a shot of adrenaline hits my heart. I pop out of bed and miraculously I can take a morning routine that usually takes me 30 minutes and condense it to only 3 minutes. It's just a mass chaos of clothes flying and cologne spraying in that small time frame. Of course then you have to explain at work why you were late. It makes for such a wonderful day. At least we always have that old alarm clock to blame!

Good Night

Are there times when you are so tired, you can't fall asleep? Some try counting sheep or reciting the alphabet. This doesn't work for me. What I have found is that two shots of vodka and a sleeping pill go a long ways to reaching that nice slumber you've been dreaming about. Or you could just start reading my book. Good night folks!

A Final Thought

We are only on this earth for a blink of an eye. Make the most of it! You never know when your time will be up or when you might lose a loved one. We should all live each day like it's our last and appreciate all that God has given us.

Never be afraid to try something new. Never be afraid to set a high goal and go for it. If you don't, you might regret it later in life.

Nothing to it, but to do it.

Thomas C. Brogan

Thomas Brogan was born July 12, 1978 in Des Moines, Iowa.

Thomas is described by his friends as easy going, creative, sarcastic and generally a "nice guy". His sarcastic side can really be seen throughout his writing. Thomas likes to find the humor in everyday life and not take life too seriously.

Some of his favorite things include traveling, spending time with family, drinking tea, eating new foods and trying to solve the world's problems.

Do you want more Brogan?
www.broganbook.com

YOUR THOUGHTS

(Use this space to write down what's on your mind.)